For Baby Megan, with love

Designed by Louise Millar

Printed in China
for the publishers Piccadilly Press Ltd.,
5 Castle Road, London NW1 8PR

ISBN: 978 1 85340 761 1 (paperback)
978 1 85340 766 6 (hardback)

5 7 9 10 8 6 4

Set in Bembo 30pt

A catalogue record for this book is available from the British Library

Other books in the TOFFEE series:

  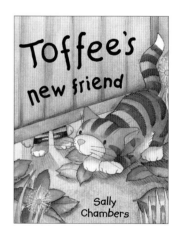

TOFFEE IN TROUBLE	TOFFEE TAKES A NAP	TOFFEE'S NEW FRIEND
ISBN: 978 1 85340 594 5	ISBN: 978 1 85340 617 1	ISBN: 978 1 85340 654 6
(p/b)	(p/b)	(p/b)

Toffee's night noises

Sally Chambers

Piccadilly Press • London

It is almost dark.
The sun is sinking in the sky
and soon it will be night.
Toffee loves the night.

Everyone is getting
ready for bed.

The windows are shut.
Thump! Thump!

The curtains are
closed.
Swish! Swish!

The doors are locked.
Clink! Clink!

Teeth are
cleaned.
Brush!
Brush!

Lights are
turned out.
Click! Click!

Goodnight, Mum!
Goodnight, Dad!
Goodnight, Toffee!

The house is very quiet.
Everyone is sleeping.

But the garden is full of sounds.
All the night creatures are waking up.

The moths are humming
around the light.

Hrr!
Hrr!
Hrr!
Hrr!

Toffee loves to watch the moths.

The mice are out too.
Toffee can hear them
under the shed.
Scratch! Scratch! Scratch!

And the owl is
calling to the moon.
Twit-twoo
Twit-twooo.

The traffic rumbles on
all through the night.
The clock chimes to
tell the time.
The town is never quiet.

It is very late. Suddenly Toffee hears a strange sound.

What can it be?
Toffee keeps
very still.

Then there is
an even
louder noise.

Crash!

Bang!

Clatter!

Toffee quickly climbs the tree.

Woof! Woof! Woof!

It is only the dog next door.
"Max!" calls a voice.
Then it is quiet again.

It is just before dawn.
The garden is almost silent.
Even the moon
looks sleepy.

The sun is starting to rise.
The birds are singing to
welcome the day.
There are voices.
The dustmen have arrived.

The bins *crash* and
the lorry *whirrs*,
munching the load.

The night noises have gone.
And now it is morning.

Then there is a sound Toffee loves.

Toffee!